# Friends Forever

*Six Stories Celebrating the Joys of Friendship*

Written by Debbie Butcher Wiersma
and Veveca Gustafson
Illustrated by Samuel J. Butcher

A GOLDEN BOOK • NEW YORK
Western Publishing Company, Inc., Racine, Wisconsin 53404

*Christy and Rachel were best friends.*

# FRIENDS FOREVER

**C**hristy and Rachel were best friends. They'd been best friends since they were babies.

They took their first wobbly steps together.

And when they said their first words, they spoke to each other. They both said "Hi" and giggled, then gave each other a great big hug.

Every day Christy and Rachel played together. They shared their favorite toys and dolls. They shared their most secret of secrets. They went for wonderful walks and had lots of just-the-two-of-us talks. In the summer they went swimming, in the winter they went sledding, and in the springtime they picked beautiful flowers to make Easter bouquets.

Christy and Rachel always said, "We have such happy times together. We'll be best friends forever."

*Rachel always seemed to know just how Christy was feeling.*

But one day Christy was not her usual happy self. Her face looked so sad.

"What's wrong?" Rachel asked as she helped Christy with her hair. "I can tell something is making you sad."

Rachel always seemed to know just how Christy was feeling. And that day Christy looked like she was feeling really awful.

"Something *is* wrong," the little blond girl said. "I *am* sad. Something very sad is about to happen."

"What can I do to help?" Rachel asked. "Helping is what friends are for."

"I don't think you can help this time, Rachel," Christy said with a sniff. "Mommy says we're moving soon. My family is moving far away."

"Very far?" Rachel asked. Her heart sank, and she felt a big lump in her throat. She wanted to make Christy feel better. But now Rachel was feeling sad, too.

"Very, very far," Christy said as a tear trickled down her cheek.

Rachel tried to be brave. But Christy could see that her news had made Rachel sad.

The next morning, even before they had a chance to say "Hello," the friends were crying together. Rachel gave Christy a hug and said, "What will I ever do without you?"

*Rachel gave Christy a hug…*

The girls spent every day together for the next three weeks. And then it was time to go. The day the moving van pulled out of her friend's driveway was the saddest day of Rachel's life. She didn't want to play. She didn't want to talk. She wouldn't even eat her dinner. The sad little girl went to bed that night with tears on her cheeks and a lonely feeling in her heart.

"I know how sad you are," Rachel's mother told her the next day. "But I also know you *will* feel better. Maybe the people who move into Christy's house will have a little girl for you to play with."

But Rachel didn't want another friend, and she didn't want to sit and watch strangers move into Christy's house. She decided to go for a walk to her favorite park. How could she ever have fun without Christy? She tossed a coin into a wishing well and heard it plop in the water.

She looked deep down into the well water. "I wish you were here, Christy," she whispered to her own reflection.

Rachel began to remember how much fun she and Christy used to have making up wishes and pretending they would always come true. These happy memories made her smile.

*She tossed a coin into a wishing well.*

"I didn't think I'd ever smile again," she said to herself. "If happy memories can make you smile, then I should write some down and send them to Christy."

At that very same time, in her new backyard, Christy was looking into the water in a beautiful birdbath. It reminded her of the wishing well in her favorite park in her old neighborhood. She smiled as she remembered the wishing games she used to play with Rachel.

"I think I'll write a letter to my friend," said Christy. "I wouldn't want her to forget all of our fun times."

That day the girls wrote long letters to each other, remembering the same good times they'd had together.

The happiness they felt when they read each other's letters made Christy and Rachel realize that they didn't need to live next door to be forever friends.

*At that very same time...Christy was looking into the water...*

# GOOD FRIENDS NEVER DRIFT APART

A long time ago there were two Indian tribes separated by a clear blue lake. A little boy named Tonka lived on one side of the lake, and a little girl named Shonnie lived on the other.

Tonka and Shonnie were best friends. Every day Tonka would paddle his canoe over to Shonnie's camp. Their days were filled with laughter as they played hide-and-seek, canoed in the lake, or just daydreamed on a soft, grassy hill.

The bigger boys in Tonka's tribe liked to play hunting games all day, but Tonka preferred to go hiking with Shonnie.

The bigger girls in Shonnie's tribe liked to pretend that they were mothers with their baby dolls. Shonnie had more fun trying to catch frogs with Tonka.

*A little boy named Tonka lived on one side of the lake . . .*

Every morning the little Indian girl would wait for Tonka on her side of the lake. But one morning Tonka didn't see his friend anywhere—the grassy bank was empty. He got out of his canoe and walked up to Shonnie's tepee.

"Helloooo," he called.

"Shhhh!" a voice said from inside. Shonnie slipped outside. "Hello, Tonka," she said. "I'm sorry, but I can't play today. Mommy needs help with our new baby."

Tonka didn't know what to say. They always played together… every day. He waved good-bye and dragged his feet back to his little canoe.

"Poor Shonnie," he thought. "I bet she wishes she could be playing instead of staying home with that baby."

Tonka tried to catch frogs. He hiked up a little hill. He even tried to play hunting games like the big boys. Nothing seemed to be much fun. He sat on his favorite daydreaming hill and thought, "I bet Shonnie is awfully lonely. Being stuck with that baby all day can't be any fun. I'll send her a smoke signal to say hello."

*...and a little girl named Shonnie lived on the other.*

Tonka felt a little better after sending her a message, so he headed off for his own camp with a little skip and a hop.

"Oh, Tonka," called his mother. "I've been wondering where you were. I need some help, and all the big boys are gone."

"Shonnie couldn't play today, so I don't have anything to do," Tonka said. "What do you need my help with?"

"Well, it's usually a job for a bigger boy," said his mother. "But I'm sure you can help. We need extra wood for the special bonfire tonight."

Tonka was really excited. He had never been asked to do big boys' work before. When his mother called him for dinner that night, the camp's woodpile was stacked up so high that Tonka could hardly reach the top.

"Look what you've done!" his mother said happily. "You big strong boy. You are really growing up!"

Tonka saw the pride in her eyes as she smiled at him. He felt a very warm, happy feeling right down to his toes.

*Tonka felt a little better after sending her a message…*

The next day Tonka hurried to Shonnie's camp to tell her all about his day.

"I stacked wood from the forest *all day long,*" he told her when they met.

"Oh, you poor thing," she said. "I spent the whole day with our new baby."

That reminded Tonka of how he had felt yesterday morning. "You must have been very lonely," he said.

Shonnie smiled. "I had a wonderful day," she said. "That was the first time Mommy ever asked me to do grown-up work. It made me feel special."

Tonka smiled too. "I know how you feel," he said. "I almost felt like a grown-up myself when I was stacking all that wood."

The two friends drifted in Tonka's canoe and watched the clouds float by.

"You know what?" Shonnie said. "I think we're starting to grow up."

Tonka nodded. "And that probably means that we won't be able to play together every day."

"You may be right," Shonnie said with a big smile. "But it doesn't mean that we'll ever stop being the very best of friends!"

*The two friends drifted in Tonka's canoe…*

# A True Friend

I t was Tubby the pig's birthday. She was three years old. Every year Penny, the farmer's daughter, would give Tubby a birthday surprise.

The little pig always loved her surprises, but this year she was especially excited. Penny had promised to find a friend for Tubby.

It was hard for the little pig to make friends. Once she met a cow in the pasture.

"Hello, Mrs. Cow," Tubby said. "How are you today?"

Mrs. Cow smiled. "Just fine, thank you. It's such a beautiful day. But what is that awful smell? Oh, my goodness!" gasped the cow. "It's YOU!"

Tubby tried to make friends with the barn cat and the farmer's dog. She tried to make friends with all of the farm animals. But even the other pigs on the farm stayed away from Tubby. It seemed nobody wanted to be friends with a smelly pig. And the biggest problem was that, unlike the other pigs, Tubby truly liked being dirty. It was her favorite way to be.

But today was different. Tubby had taken a bath. She wanted to be sparkling clean when she met her new friend. And she was!

"My, oh my," said Penny. "What a beautiful pig you are!" She petted Tubby and gave her a big bite of ice cream.

*"My, oh my,"* said Penny. *"What a beautiful pig you are!"*

Tubby shared her birthday treats with all the farm animals. They didn't mind being around her now, because she was all clean. Tubby should have been happy, but she wasn't. What she really wanted was to go roll in the nice cool mud.

"I wish I didn't have to be so clean," she thought. "I don't even feel like this is *me*!"

After all the cake and ice cream were gone, Penny gave Tubby the special gift.

Tubby carefully opened the box and inside she found—a skunk!

"I'm Simon," said the skunk.

As soon as the other animals saw Simon, they ran away!

The skunk looked around and sighed. "I suppose you won't want to be my friend, either," Simon said. "Nobody ever does because they think that I will spray bad smells on them. They don't understand I only do that when I'm frightened."

But Tubby didn't care. She thought Simon smelled just wonderful. She showed Simon her pigpen, and he didn't mind a bit when Tubby rolled around in the mud all afternoon.

Tubby learned something very important that day. She learned that you can only really be yourself with your true friends, and it's no fun trying to be someone you're not!

*"I'm Simon,"* said the skunk.

# THE BEST GIFT EVER

**T**ommy the turtle had just finished cleaning and polishing his shell. Since he had already put away food for the winter, everything seemed to be in order.

The little turtle put on his best hat and tie and headed out for a nice walk in the woods.

Tommy could feel the cold air of winter coming, and it was time to say good-bye to all of his summer friends. As he walked down a leafy path in the woods, he saw some little flowers.

"Good-bye, little flowers," said the turtle. "Thank you for brightening my days. I'll see you next year."

Farther down the path Tommy stopped and looked way up high. "Good-bye, pretty leaves," he said. "Thank you for your shade in the summer and all your pretty colors in the fall. I'll see you again next spring."

When a bird flew by, Tommy tipped his hat and smiled. "Good-bye, Mrs. Robin," he said. "Have a lovely flight south. I'll see you next spring, too."

Mrs. Robin waved her wing and chirped as she flew off into the crisp morning air.

Tommy the turtle was in a very good mood. He whistled a happy little tune as he walked into a clearing in the woods.

*The little turtle put on his best hat and tie ...*

Then Tommy saw something that made his good mood disappear. He stopped whistling. Standing in the clearing was a very sad-looking mouse.

This sad little mouse looked skinny and tired and very, very cold. He had a dry piece of bread in his paws.

"Why are you standing out here in the cold?" asked Tommy. "Are you lost?"

"M-m-m-my name is M-M-Marvin," the little mouse told Tommy between shivers. "I'm not lost. I don't have anywhere to go. I don't have a home anymore."

Tommy looked at Marvin and asked, "You don't have warm clothes … or a blanket? You don't have anywhere to go?"

"No," Marvin said quietly. "I don't know anyone in this part of the woods."

Just then a snowflake landed on Tommy's nose. "Oh, my goodness!" said the turtle. "The first snow of the year. I really must be on my way. Good luck, Marvin."

*Standing in the clearing was a very sad-looking mouse.*

Tommy hurried back to his nice warm home. Then he had a big dinner and climbed into his soft bed. But he couldn't go to sleep.

He couldn't get poor Marvin out of his mind. Marvin didn't have a warm house, or a big dinner, or even a soft bed. But what could Tommy do?

And then he knew! He got right out of bed and went to his workshop. Tommy had decided to make an early Christmas present for Marvin.

He worked all that night and through the next day. He worked and worked and worked until he was finished.

Tommy wrapped his gift in pretty Christmas paper with a big ribbon on top.

Then, to make it seem a little more like Christmas, he tied pretend antlers on his head.

Tommy giggled as he left his house. He was so excited. What would Marvin think?

Tommy walked through the forest once again. This time the pond had ice at its edges. Most of the leaves had fallen off the trees, and all of the flowers were gone.

Tommy reached the clearing and looked around. "Marvin?" he called. "Where are you?"

The little turtle looked and looked, but he couldn't find Marvin. There was no mouse anywhere to be seen.

"Oh, Marvin," Tommy cried. "I took too long and now you're gone."

*… he tied pretend antlers on his head.*

Just then the turtle heard some leaves rustle. He saw a little mouse nose poking through the leaves. It looked like Marvin had burrowed under the leaves to get warm.

"I'm so happy to see you!" shouted Tommy. "Look! I made a Christmas surprise for you!"

"Th-thank you," said the cold little mouse. He smiled a tiny smile and opened his gift. Inside was a perfect mouse bed with a soft warm blanket. "And best of all," Tommy said happily, "I built a house for you RIGHT NEXT TO MINE! We're going to be neighbors! Come on. I'll take you there!"

"Oh, Tommy," the mouse cried. "It's just beautiful! It's the best surprise in the whole world! But I have nothing to give you," Marvin said quietly. "Except my friendship, but that doesn't seem like much compared to your gift to me."

"Your friendship is the best gift you could ever give me," said Tommy with a great big smile. "I couldn't think of anything that I'd rather have."

Marvin climbed into his soft warm bed and snuggled under his new blanket. In a very sleepy and very happy voice, he said, "Thank you, Friend."

Tommy smiled and headed home with his new friend.

*Marvin climbed into his soft warm bed…*

# Missy and Mr. Snowfriend

Missy loved to make believe. She would build castles out of cardboard boxes, and be the prettiest princess in the land. She would dress up in her mother's clothes and pretend she was going to a royal ball. Sometimes she played in the attic. Far in the back corner was an old trunk filled with the best things for pretending.

Her mother would always tell her, "Your imagination is a wonderful thing. As long as you use it, you will never be lonely."

Missy didn't know if that was true or not. She did feel lonely sometimes. She was feeling lonely now, because it was wintertime, and all the bigger kids on her street were in school. Missy loved to make up pretend friends, but they weren't the same as real ones. You can't hug an imaginary friend.

"I know!" thought Missy one cold, lonely morning. "I'll go outside and see if I can find a new friend!"

*Missy loved to make believe.*

She got all bundled up in her scarf, hat, mittens, and coat, and went out to play. But there were no other children to play with.

"Well, that's okay," thought Missy. "I can make a friend out of snow."

She started with a little ball of snow. She rolled it, and packed it, and smoothed it out until it was a perfect snowfriend tummy. Then she made another ball for a head and placed it on top.

Missy went back in the house to get an old hat and scarf from the attic. Finally, she put a very happy face on her snowfriend.

"Hello, Mr. Snowfriend," Missy said happily. "My name is Missy."

Missy spent the morning getting to know her new friend. They talked, and laughed, and told stories all morning long. When it was time to go inside for lunch, the little girl hugged her friend. "Mr. Snowfriend, you're my best friend! I can't wait until we can play again," Missy said.

"He really is my best friend, Mommy," she said at lunch. "And he tells me the funniest stories."

Missy's mother smiled. "I'm glad that you have someone to play with," she said. "After your nap, you can go out to play again."

*"I can make a friend out of snow."*

*"No!" cried Missy. "Don't melt away!"*

When Missy woke up, she hurried to get into her coat and
ran out to play. But what she saw made her cry. The sun had
come out and it was melting Mr. Snowfriend!

"No!" cried Missy. "Don't melt away! You're my best friend!"

But Mr. Snowfriend kept melting ... drip, drip, drip ... until
all that was left was slush.

"Oh, Mommy," cried the sad little girl. "What will I do? My
snowfriend melted away!"

Her mother hugged her and said, "It's supposed to snow
tonight, so you can make a new friend tomorrow."

Missy knew that she couldn't do that. Mr. Snowfriend was
special. She didn't ever want any other snowfriend.

That night Missy looked out at the stars. Quietly she began to sing a little song that she had made up.

*"Little angels, small and bright,*
*Hear me when I cry tonight.*
*I wish I may, I wish I might*
*Have my snowfriend back tonight."*

Much later, when Missy was fast asleep, snowflakes began to fall from the sky. And with them came two little angels.

"Be very quiet," one said to the other as he gathered up some snow. "We don't want to wake her."

The angels worked quickly and soon Mr. Snowfriend was all put back together.

One little angel lifted the snowfriend's hat and put a secret surprise underneath.

*The angels worked quickly...*

The next morning Missy looked out her window. "Mr. Snowfriend!" she yelled happily. "You're back!

"Oh, Mr. Snowfriend," she said as she threw her arms around him. "We can play all day again!" The snowfriend smiled at her with a twinkle in his eye.

As the two friends played, the day grew longer and the sun shone brighter. Soon the snowfriend began to melt again.

A tear appeared in Missy's eye. "I guess you'll never stay forever," she said. She sat down in the snow and cried.

When she looked up again, there was nothing left but a lopsided pile of snow with a hat on top. Missy reached for the hat. "I'll keep this to remember all the fun we had," she said.

But when she lifted the hat, something tumbled to the ground. It was a tiny glass ball with a bow around it. She lifted the ball gently and looked inside. There was Mr. Snowfriend in his hat and scarf. He was wearing the biggest smile. And when she shook the ball, snow floated down on Mr. Snowfriend.

Missy knew that this time her friend would stay forever. Mr. Snowfriend would never melt again.

She looked up into the bright blue sky and said, "It's just beautiful. Thank you, little angels. Thank you."

*Mr. Snowfriend would never melt again.*

# WADDLE *I* DO WITHOUT YOU?

arah looked forward to the warmest days of the summer. That was the time of year when she went to visit her grandfather on his farm.

There were always so many wonderful things to see and do. Bluebirds flew in the open fields, bright flowers grew everywhere, and there were more trees on the farm than Sarah had ever seen in the city where she lived.

As she walked down to the pond, Sarah said, "It's so wonderful here. I just wish I had a friend to share it with."

But there were no other boys and girls at the pond. Sarah sat down on an old tree stump by the water and took off her shoes and socks.

"Wading in the water would be a lot more fun if I had a friend," she said.

She walked through the cool water and smiled as tiny fish nipped at her toes. Birds were chirping all around, and Sarah was just thinking how peaceful it was when...

*SPLASH!* Up flew a lily pad! A very wet goose was under it. The goose splashed its wings in the water and wiggled its tail. It seemed very happy to see someone else in the pond.

Sarah was not too happy at all. She was covered with water. "Oh, look what you've done!" she told the goose. "You've gotten me all wet! Now go away, little goose."

*The goose splashed its wings ... and wiggled its tail.*

The goose stopped splashing and looked sadly at the little girl, as if to say, "I was only playing." It waddled up to Sarah and flapped its wings more gently, making little waves in the water.

Sarah shook her head. "No, I don't want to play with a messy wet goose. Go away!" she said.

With that she stomped up to the shore and plopped down on the grass. But the goose sat down next to her. It looked at Sarah with its big blue eyes. Sarah could almost hear it saying, "Please don't go. Stay and play with me. Be my friend."

"But I don't want a silly goose for a friend," said the little girl.

Sarah stood up and walked toward her grandfather's house. But the goose wouldn't give up. It kept following her, nipping at her apron. Sarah started to giggle.

Finally she turned and said, "I know you want to be my friend, little goose. But go find another goose like yourself. I want to play with girls and boys like me. That's just how it works. Now you go back to the pond, and I'll go back to the farm."

That seemed to fix things. When Sarah continued on her way, the goose headed down a different path.

But just as she reached her grandfather's backyard, Sarah felt a little nudge on her hand. This time the goose had a beautiful flower in its bill.

"What a sweet goose you are," the little girl said.

She took the flower and gave the goose a great big hug. "And do you know what?" she said. "I think it would be fun to have a goose for a friend. Just because you're a goose and I'm a little girl doesn't mean we can't be friends!"

Even though they made an odd pair, they would still have lots of fun together playing in the pond, hiding in the tall grass, and watching the drifting clouds.

The summer had just begun for Sarah, and it was sure to be the best ever—for now she had a friend to share it with.